Danny, the Duck with No QUACK

Malachy Doyle

Janet Samuel

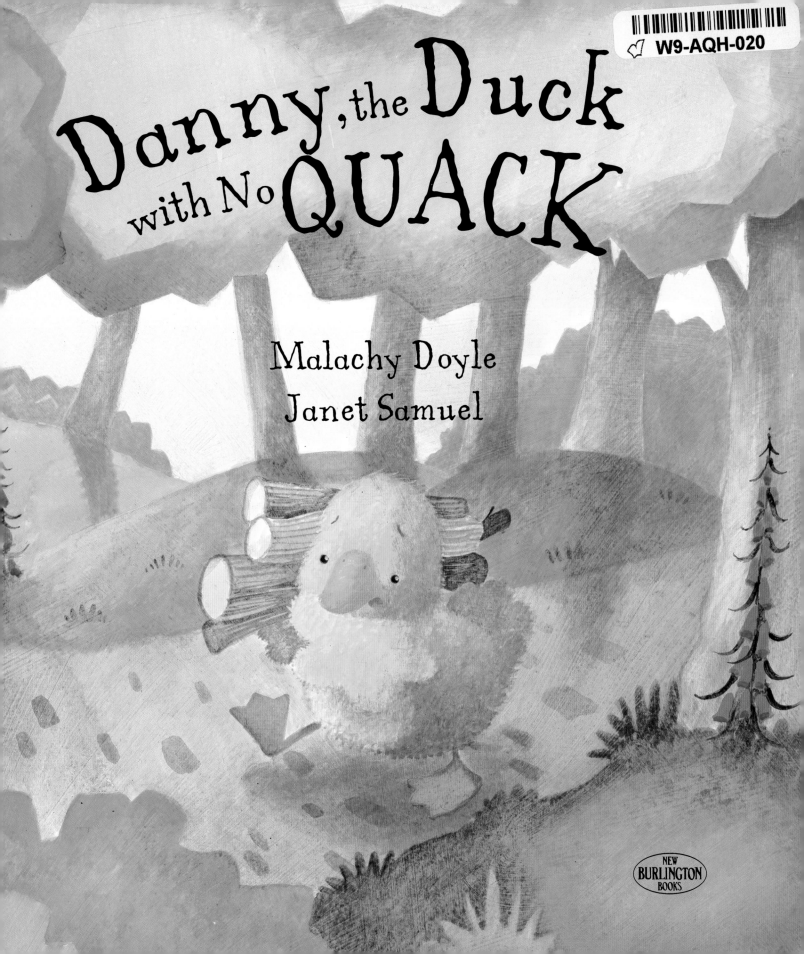

NEW BURLINGTON BOOKS

Every morning, the ducks and the hens gather in the yard for a chat.

"How's the quack, Danny?" asks a chicken. "What's the story? Tell us the news."

But Danny's a shy little duck,
and he never knows what to say.

He keeps his beak
firmly shut, bows his
head and turns away.

"Come on, Danny!" squawk the birds one day. "Don't be such a scaredy-quack! There must be something you can tell us!"

Danny swallows and opens his beak—but nothing comes out.

Not a peep, not a splutter, not a cackle, not a hoot. He's **lost his quack!**

Right, thinks Danny, that's it.
And he takes off up the lane
to find a tale worth telling.

Yes, he wanders up the track
to find his quack.

And Danny knows he shouldn't
—these are tricky-looking foxes.

He opens his beak to say that he won't.
But nothing comes out.

And Danny knows he shouldn't
—these are hungry-looking foxes.
He opens his mouth to say no.

But he
can't.

"Now who'll fill the pot with water?"
asks one fox.
"The duck with no quack,"
smirks the other.

And Danny knows he shouldn't
—these are scary-looking foxes.

He opens his beak as wide as he
can, and what does he say?

Nothing.

"The duck with no quack!" cries the other, jumping up.

They rush toward Danny and they're just about to grab him, when...

He throws himself to the side
of the pot.

The two foxes are so surprised,
they tumble right inside!

"How's the quack, Danny?" ask the other ducks,
when he rushes back to the farmyard.
"Yeah, what's the cluck, duck?" ask the hens.

And aren't they all
amazed to hear
Danny quacking?

Aren't they all
astonished at the
tale he has to tell?

"Go away!" cluck the angry hens.

"And don't come back!" quack the ducks.

And Danny's quack is the loudest.

"Quackity-quack!" he says. "Don't come back!"

QUACK!

Notes for parents and teachers

- After you have read this book with a child or children, there are many ways you can extend their interest in and enjoyment of the story.

- At the start of the story, the ducks and hens have a chat. Ask the children what they would talk about. Then ask them to chat together as though they are the birds.

- Ask the children to act out the whole story. One is Danny, two are the foxes, and the others are the farmyard birds and animals. Ask them to move and talk like the characters would move and talk. Then ask the children how they feel.

- Danny is a shy little duck. Ask the children if they know anyone who they think is shy and what it would feel like. Can they think of a time when they felt particularly shy? When was it and what happened?

- Ask the children to pretend to be Danny and tell the story from his point of view. For example, "I'm a shy little duck and I often don't know what to say..." Then they can pretend to be one of the foxes and tell the story from his point of view. For example, "One day I was in the wood with my friend and I found a pot..."

- Help the children to make hand puppets of Danny and the two foxes out of paper bags, old gloves, or old socks. They can then use the puppets to reenact the story.

- With the children, make a map of Danny's journey. Draw or write what happened along the way. Ask the children to point to where each event took place as you retell the story.

- Ask the children to list the four things the foxes asked Danny to do. How many did he do, and why didn't he do the last one?

- When the foxes ask Danny to carry the pot, he knows he should say no but he can't find the words. Have any of the children ever wanted to say no but were not able to? What did they wish they had said or done?

- Do the children think Danny had changed by the end of the story? How and why has he changed?

- Did anyone feel sorry for the foxes ending up in the pot? Do they think the ducks and hens should have left them there? Why do they think the ducks and hens let them out?

A NEW BURLINGTON BOOK
The Old Brewery
6 Blundell Street
London N7 9BH

Copyright © QEB Publishing, Inc. 2009

Published in the United States by
QEB Publishing, Inc.
3 Wrigley, Suite A
Irvine, CA 92618

www.qed-publishing.co.uk

ISBN 978 1 60992 864 3

Library of Congress Cataloging-in-Publication Data

Doyle, Malachy.
  Danny, the duck with no quack / by Malachy Doyle ; illustrated by Janet Samuel.
    p. cm. -- (QEB storytime)
  Summary: Shy little Danny the duck goes in search of his missing quack, only to find that it takes two tricky foxes to solve the problem.
  ISBN 978-1-60992-125-5 (paperback)
  [1. Ducks--Fiction. 2. Bashfulness--Fiction. 3. Adventure and adventurers--Fiction.] I. Samuel, Janet, ill. II. Title.

PZ7.D775Dan 2010
[E]--dc22

2009001994

sPrinted in China

Author Malachy Doyle
Illustrator Janet Samuel
Designer Alix Wood
Project Editor Heather Amery

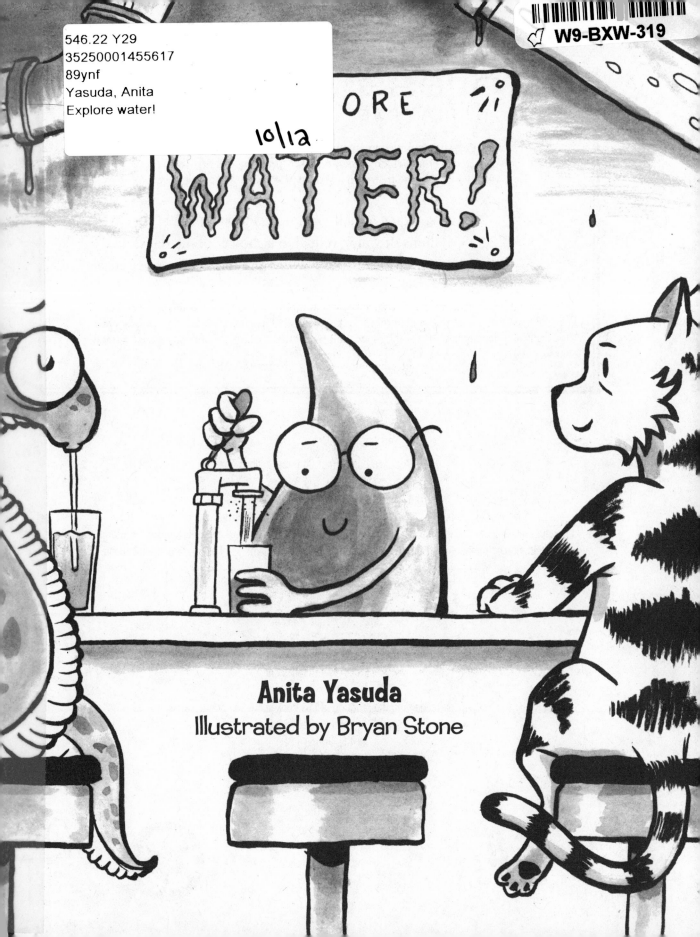

ORE
WATER!

Anita Yasuda

Illustrated by Bryan Stone

green press INITIATIVE

Nomad Press is committed to preserving ancient forests and natural resources. We elected to print *Explore Water!* on 100% post consumer recycled paper, processed chlorine free. As a result, for this printing, we have saved:

24 Trees, (equal to half an American football field)

22,958 Gallons of water, (equal to a shower of 4.8 days)

7,544 Pounds of air emissions, (equal to emissions of 1 car per year)

Nomad Press made this paper choice because our printer, Transcontinental, is a member of Green Press Initiative, a nonprofit program dedicated to supporting authors, publishers, and suppliers in their efforts to reduce their use of fiber obtained from endangered forests.

For more information, visit www.greenpressinitiative.org

Nomad Press
A division of Nomad Communications
10 9 8 7 6 5 4 3 2 1

This book was manufactured by Transcontinental Gagné,
Louiseville Québec, Canada
June 2011, Job #44746
ISBN: 978-1-936313-42-6

Illustrations by Bryan Stone

Questions regarding the ordering of this book should be addressed to
Independent Publishers Group
814 N. Franklin St.
Chicago, IL 60610
www.ipgbook.com

Nomad Press
2456 Christian St.
White River Junction, VT 05001
www.nomadpress.net

CONTENTS

Titles in the **Explore Your World!** Series

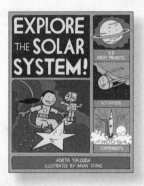

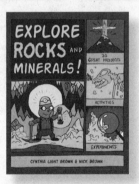

EXPLORE WATER

CAN YOU GUESS WHO I AM? I have been here since Earth began. I splash and spill. I drip and drop. You use me, play in me, and drink me. I can run through your fingers, be hard as a rock, and turn invisible. I flow through your body and history. I guided explorers and helped the first settlers. Can you guess who I am? Water!

Water is amazing. More than half of the world's animals and plants live in it. There would be no past, present, or future people without water. In fact, you would not be here. You surely would not be reading this book. And yet, we often take water for granted. But this is a mistake. We are lucky to have water. Earth is the only planet in our solar system with liquid water.

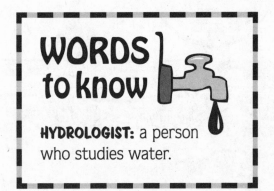

WORDS to know

HYDROLOGIST: a person who studies water.

Put on your **HYDROLOGIST** hat! A hydrologist is a person who studies water. In the following pages, you'll read about the water cycle, rain harvesting, water power, water technology, and how to use water wisely. You'll also discover how much water there is on Earth and why it falls from the sky.

Along the way you're going to do lots of fun projects, play games, do experiments, and hear some silly jokes. Be warned though, you're going to get very wet as you drip, drop, splash, and splash around.

Ready? Let's Explore Water!

JOIN THE TIME WARP TOUR

Imagine travelling through time to the beginning of Earth. Hop on, our tour bus is leaving now for the very distant past. Take a look around. This is Earth 4½ billion years ago. Of course, it's very different. Earth begins as a hot swirling mass of gas, rock, and dust.

OUR BLUE PLANET

What if you were an astronaut in a spaceship high above Earth? From space, Earth looks like a bright blue gumball!

Looking closer, you can spot the five Great Lakes of North America, the dark lines of the Amazon River, and the bright blue of the oceans. No matter where you look, you see water. This is not surprising, because water covers 70 percent of Earth. It is in the puddles on your street and in the streams near your home. It is even in the air.

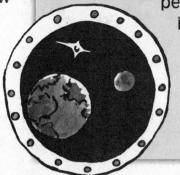

WORDS to know

COMET: a ball of ice and dust that **ORBITS** the sun.

ORBIT: circle around something.

METEOR: a rock that orbits the sun.

WATER VAPOR: water as a gas, like steam or mist.

EROSION: the wearing down of the earth's surface.

METEOROLOGIST: a scientist who studies weather patterns.

Later, these parts come together to form a huge glowing ball. Look out for the **COMETS** and **METEORS** falling from the sky above!

There is water trapped inside the earth. As the earth's center heats up, **WATER VAPOR** rises to the surface. Get out your umbrellas! When the earth starts to cool, that water vapor turns into liquid, or rain. For millions of years it rains.

Meanwhile, huge land masses smash together like bumper cars—*craaaash!*—and then split apart. The falling rain collects in the empty, low-lying areas. This is how oceans begin.

The amount of water on Earth will remain the same. As Earth cools and warms, water will freeze, thaw, and carve the surface. This is **EROSION**. Eventually, the earth's land and water forms will begin to look familiar to you.

Do you think the earth is exactly the same now as when you were born? It is not, because land and water forms are always moving! For example, oceans are always changing shape. The Atlantic Ocean widens a few inches every year. How can we tell this? Scientists measure the distances between landmarks on the ocean floor.

JUST 4 LAUGHS!

What kind of meteor can tell the weather? **A METEOROLOGIST.**

OCEANS

We use the oceans, all five of them. These are the Arctic, Atlantic, Pacific, Indian, and Southern (Antarctic) Oceans. The oceans are a source of food, energy, and raw materials, such as sand. Oceans are a watery highway for ships. They're fun to play in, too!

WORDS to know

RESERVOIR: an area that holds water.

CONTINENT: a large land mass.

CURRENT: the constant movement of water in a direction.

EQUATOR: an invisible line circling the globe, halfway between the North and South Poles.

Oceans are the earth's largest water **RESERVOIRS**. They cover about three-quarters of the earth's surface, or 140 million square miles (360 million square kilometers). If that sounds huge, it is. All seven **CONTINENTS** could fit in the Pacific Ocean alone!

Wind, waves, and **CURRENTS** keep oceans constantly in motion. There are no walls between oceans, so currents move ocean water all around the world. It's like a global conveyer belt. Deep, cold water moves south across the ocean floor as warm surface water from the **EQUATOR** moves north. It can take 1,000 years to finish the cycle! This is how currents heat and cool our planet.

SALT WATER

Have you ever seen a movie where people are floating in a lifeboat? When they drink water from the ocean, they quickly spit it out. *Yuck!* Why is this? Ocean water is just too salty for people. Most of Earth's water is undrinkable salt water—97 percent to be exact. But salt water is just right for many creatures. Birds, snails, and the largest animal on the planet, the blue whale, all call salt water home.

Why is the sea so salty? No one picked up a giant salt shaker and shook it into the ocean. When it rains, water flows over the land and picks up minerals. Salt is one of these minerals. Eventually the water flows into the ocean. Over time the oceans get saltier and saltier. If you could spread it all over the earth, the ocean salt would be 500 feet thick (152 meters). That's the height of a 40-story office building!

Lake Assal, in Africa, is the saltiest lake in the world. It is 10 times saltier than an ocean. Most of the water has dried up because it's so hot—up to 126 degrees Fahrenheit (52 degrees Celsius). This leaves behind the salt.

AMAZING OCEAN FACTS

◊ The deepest point in the ocean is the Mariana Trench in the Pacific Ocean. At 36,000 feet deep (11 kilometers), the trench is deeper than Mount Everest is high!

◊ The top 10 feet (3 meters) of the ocean holds as much heat as all the air surrounding Earth.

◊ Less than 10 percent of the oceans have been explored.

◊ 99 percent of Earth's living space is ocean.

◊ The Pacific Ocean is the largest body of water. It has twice as much water as the Atlantic Ocean.

FRESHWATER

We all need freshwater to live. After playing outside, you grab a drink of water. *Glug, glug, glug.* You don't give it a second thought. But freshwater isn't as common as you think.

Only 3 percent of all the water in the world is fresh. Most of this water is out of reach. Almost all of it is found in **ICE CAPS**, **GLACIERS**, and underground. Only 1 percent of all freshwater is available for us to drink.

WORDS to know

ICE CAP: a thick layer of permanent ice.

GLACIER: a huge mass of ice and snow.

ECOSYSTEM: a community of plants and animals living in an area, relying on each other to survive.

Where else can freshwater be found?

* Water vapor in the air.

* Rain, snow, sleet, and hail.

* Surface water that collects in rivers, lakes, or wetlands.

* Groundwater found in cracks and spaces underground.

Rivers, streams, ponds, and lakes are freshwater **ECOSYSTEMS**. But have you heard of prairie potholes? Few people have—unless they live in Canada, Minnesota, or the Dakotas. Prairie potholes fill with melted snow and rain in the spring. They are important rest stops for migrating birds.

FROZEN

More than two-thirds of Earth's freshwater is frozen. Ice caps and glaciers hold the bulk of this water. Ice caps are permanent sheets of ice found around the poles. In the south, the Antarctic ice sheet is about 40 million years old. It rests on land. In the north, the Arctic ice cap floats on water. It rotates around the North Pole, taking four years to make one rotation.

WORDS to know

METEOROLOGY: the study of weather and **CLIMATE**.

CLIMATE: average weather patterns in an area over a long period of time.

WHO LIVES WHERE?

Do you know which animals live in salt or freshwater? Test your knowledge. For each of the following animals write down whether they live in freshwater or salt water. Then compare your answers to the answer key below this box.

A. Emperor Penguin

B. Crocodile

C. Hippopotamus

D. Gray Whale

Answers: A/Salt, B/Fresh, C/Fresh, D/Salt

Glaciers begin life as a snowflake. Unlike the snowflakes you catch on your tongue, these snowflakes don't melt. The layers upon layers of snow slowly turn to ice. Over hundreds of years this ice, along with sediment and rock, press together.

Glaciers are on every continent except Australia. Most are found in Greenland and Antarctica. Alaska has thousands of glaciers, some as big as a football field and others miles long! The longest glacier in North America is the Bering Glacier. It is 127 miles long (204 kilometers).

Meet A Scientist

JOANNE SIMPSON (1923–2010) was the first woman in America to earn a PhD in **METEOROLOGY**. She also built the first computer model of clouds.

7

Water Forms

Land and water forms cover the surface of the earth. They create the overall shape of the earth. Now you can make your own water form using clay. Here are some of the most common water forms.

RIVER: a small body of flowing water.

BAY: an area of water ringed by land on three sides.

LAKE: a large body of water, usually freshwater.

STRAIT: a narrow body of water between two pieces of land. It joins two larger bodies of water.

OCEAN: the salty water that covers most of the earth's surface.

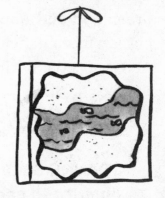

1 Choose a water form. Look in books or online for images.

2 Open a CD case. This will be your base. Thinly cover your base with one color of modeling clay.

3 Select a contrasting color to create a water form. Add clay fish and plants. Close the CD case.

4 Attach the string with tape to the back and hang up your water form.

Things to Notice

≈ **What plants grow near or in your water form?**

≈ **What kind of wildlife lives in your water form?**

≈ **What pollutants could enter your water form?**

Salt Water Experiment

Trapped in the middle of the ocean with no freshwater to drink? No problem! There is a way to make salt water good to drink.

1 Fill a bowl with a few of inches of water and mix in two large spoonfuls of salt.

2 Place the heavy mug in the bowl. Stretch plastic wrap across the top of the whole bowl. Secure it with a rubber band. Place a stone in the middle of the plastic.

3 Place the bowl in the sunlight. The next day check how much water is in the cup. Taste the water.

Things to Notice

≈ What happened to the salt?

≈ Why is the plastic wrap important?

≈ What else did you notice about this experiment?

Supplies

mixing bowl

water

table salt

large spoon

heavy mug, smaller than the mixing bowl

plastic wrap

rubber band

small rock

Glacier on the Move

Supplies

dish towel

cookie sheet

sweetened shredded coconut

mini marshmallows

chocolate chips

vanilla ice cream

notebook and pencil

camera (optional)

One million years ago, glaciers filled Yosemite National Park, California. As they moved, they cut away at the mountainsides and created the deep valleys you see today. Now you can create a glacier in your kitchen!

1 Fold a dish towel and place it under one edge of the cookie sheet to create a slope.

2 Lightly cover the cookie sheet in shredded coconut.

3 Scatter mini marshmallows and chocolate chips on different areas of the sheet.

4 Place a big scoop of ice cream at the top of the slope.

5 Write down your observations over a 15-minute period. You can take photos too if you like. Now it is time to dig in!

Things to Notice

≈ Why does the slope help the glacier?

≈ What do glaciers in nature pick up as they move?

≈ What would be in the way of a glacier's path?

W IS FOR WATER

WORDS to know

MATTER: anything that takes up space and has mass.

ATOM: the smallest unit of an **ELEMENT**.

ELEMENT: a pure substance that contains only one kind of atom.

LET'S MAKE A LIST OF THINGS THAT ARE MADE OF MATTER. An eraser. A desk. A running shoe. We'd better stop, because everything has to go on that list. Everything is **MATTER**.

Inside matter are teeny tiny building blocks called **ATOMS**. You cannot see atoms, even using a powerful microscope. There wasn't even proof that atoms existed until 1905. Atoms are so small that you can't cut them in half.

Now put on your hydrologist thinking cap. Pour a glass of tap water. How many atoms do you think are in one glass of water? The exact number is pretty hard to figure out. Now imagine counting all the stars in the universe. That would be a crazy amount! Well that glass of tap water you poured has more atoms in it than there are stars in the universe! *Atomazing!*

IN THE SPOTLIGHT

Welcome to the Circus of Substances! In the center ring is pure water. There is nothing like water. Water might be odorless, tasteless, and colorless, but it's the most important substance on Earth. All living things need water to live.

Water exists in three different forms—solid, liquid, and gas. Water can transform from one form to another and then back again. It's like magic!

At the Circus of Substances you wait for water to transform. You wait and wait. The crowd is getting restless. So why isn't anything happening? Well, water doesn't really transform by magic. It needs a change in temperature to help it along.

Luckily, the ringmaster of this circus is temperature. When temperature enters, the show can begin! First, temperature makes the room freezing cold, turning water into solid ice. Then *presto!* Temperature makes it warmer, melting the ice and transforming it into a liquid. And finally—*shazam!*—temperature makes it very hot. Now watch as water turns into a gas. *Ta dah!*

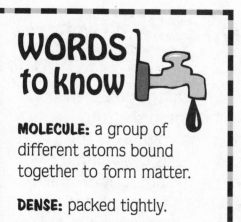

WORDS to know

MOLECULE: a group of different atoms bound together to form matter.

DENSE: packed tightly.

BRRRRRR

Roughly 2 percent of all of Earth's water can be found in ice caps, glaciers, and other forms of snow and ice. Water **MOLECULES** lock into position when they freeze.

Maybe you have noticed that the water in an ice cube tray expands when it freezes. Ice takes up more space than the liquid water it's made from. It is less **DENSE** and lighter. This is why an ice cube floats instead of sinks to the bottom of your glass.

Water is the only substance whose molecules spread out when they get colder. When other substances get colder, their molecules squish together like players in a pre-game huddle.

THE WATER MOLECULE CHEER

When atoms join together, they form molecules. A water molecule is made of three atoms. And what are those three atoms?

Give me an H! . . . Give me a 2! . . . Give me an O!

What does that spell? . . . H_2O!

The letter H stands for hydrogen. The number two shows that there are two hydrogen atoms. The letter O stands for an oxygen atom. Hydrogen and oxygen are two elements.

MINI-EXPERIMENT

A Greek scientist named Archimedes discovered why things float. While taking a bath, he saw that the water level rose as he got in the tub. "Eureka!" he shouted. He realized that the volume of the water that rose, or was displaced, equals the volume of the object in the water. Volume is the amount of space taken up by something. If the weight of the object is less than the weight of the displaced water, the object will float.

EUREKA!

Now it's time for fun! Make hollow boats of all shapes and sizes out of clay. Float them in a tub of water. Now try to sink the boats by filling them with pebbles. If your boat is lighter than the water it displaces, it floats. If it weighs more, it will sink.

DRIP DROP

When water is frozen, it doesn't move. But when water is a liquid, it sure gets around. If a water molecule could speak it might say, "See ya!" as it slips past one molecule, only to slide into another.

What happens when you pour water into containers with different shapes? The water quickly takes the shape of each container. Liquid water can bend and twist forward and back, until it fills every space!

WHOOSH!

When a pot of water boils away on the stove, you can see lots of little bubbles. How did they get there? They were there the whole time. Those bubbles are water as a gas. When water is heated, its molecules start to move very, very fast. They zoom and zip and spread way out into the air, where they become water vapor.

Water vapor is very important to Earth as a **GREENHOUSE GAS**. A greenhouse gas traps heat. Without water vapor, Earth would be very cold. The average temperature on Earth is 59 degrees Fahrenheit (15 degrees Celsius). Without water vapor, the average temperature would be 0 degrees Fahrenheit (-18 degrees Celsius).

WORDS to know

GREENHOUSE GAS: a gas in the **ATMOSPHERE** that traps heat. We need some greenhouse gases, but too many trap too much heat.

ATMOSPHERE: all of the air around the earth.

THEN+NOW

THEN: In the past, dowsing was a type of fortune-telling used to find underground water. A dowser walked around with a forked stick. When the stick twitched or dipped, it showed that water was nearby.

NOW: Today, groundwater is found using rock, mineral, and soil information. The landscape gives clues about where water can be found.

MOVING UP

WORDS to know

CAPILLARY ACTION: the way water pulls itself up into another material.

SURFACE TENSION: when water molecules on the surface pull together, creating tension.

Whoops, you just spilled a glass of water. No worries. You grab a paper towel and soak up the spilled water. This is **CAPILLARY ACTION** at work. Water molecules move into the spaces of other materials because they are "sticky."

Sticky water? Yes, you read it right. Water molecules like to hang out together. And they like to follow each other, even against gravity. "OK, we are moving on up guys," they seem to shout to each other as they travel up plant roots or fill in the spaces of a paper towel. If water molecules didn't like to stick together, there would be no raindrops. Instead, water would simply spread out.

WATER'S SKIN

Can you walk across a pond? No. But tiny aquatic insects called water striders can. **SURFACE TENSION** lets them do this. The water molecules on the pond's surface pull together. This stops them from breaking up. They pull so hard that a very thin "skin" forms. Water striders take advantage of this skin, or tension, to scoot across.

Change Your State

Supplies

a group of friends
(the bigger the better)

a large open space

In this game, you and your friends are water molecules. One person plays the scientist and the rest try to reach the scientist before getting out.

1. At the start, all kids form a line at least 15 feet (5 meters) away from the scientist.

MOLECULES

SCIENTIST

2. The scientist faces away from kids and says, "liquid." Each player must link arms with one other player and move towards the scientist.

3. The scientist may then say "solid," count to five, and turn around. Players must link arms with at least four others and shake. If the scientist sees any players not in a group of at least five, they are all out.

4. Play resumes when the scientists turns back around and says "liquid" or "gas." Gas means that the temperature is rising quickly. Players must spread out in all directions.

5. The scientist wins if all the players are out before anyone is able to touch him/her. Otherwise, the first player to touch the scientist wins the game and is the scientist for the next game.

LIQUID!

SOLID!

GAS!

Who is Faster?

In this experiment, you will discover if water molecules really do move faster when heated up.

1 With the pin, poke a hole in the bottom of two paper cups. Balance each cup in a glass.

2 Fill one cup with ice water and the other with very hot water.

3 Watch which cup leaks water faster.

Things to Notice

≈ Before you started, what did you think was going to happen?

≈ Did your experiment prove or disprove that heat makes molecules move faster?

Meet A Scientist

AGNES POCKELS (1862–1935) loved science. She did experiments in her kitchen. While studying the surface tension of water, Agnes made the first device to measure it.

Capillary Action

Here is a fun way to see water move uphill and down. It's not magic—it's capillary action!

1 Place two glasses on a table and fill one three-quarters full with water. The other one remains empty.

2 Twist a paper towel tightly and place one end in the glass with water and the other end in the empty glass.

3 Watch what happens over a 2-hour period. Write down your results.

Things to Notice

≈ **Before you began the experiment, what did you think would happen?**

≈ **What happened to the paper towel?**

≈ **What happened to the empty cup?**

Supplies

2 glasses

water

paper towel

notebook

pencil

CLEAN WATER TECH

The PlayPump is a playground toy that looks like a merry-go-round. But it's more than just a toy! The PlayPump uses energy from children playing on it to pump underground water into a storage tank above ground. This is important in rural areas of Africa where there is not enough clean water.

WATER CYCLE

THE WATER CYCLE IS HAPPENING EVERYWHERE! It's under your feet, in the air, at the beach, and even in the toilet! Freezing and thawing. Appearing and disappearing. Dripping and dropping. Water constantly circulates as a solid, liquid, or a gas. Where does water come from and where does it go? Under the ground! Into the air! Over the land! All of these answers are correct.

The total amount of water on Earth and in the atmosphere does not change. It has not changed since before dinosaurs roamed the earth. While the amount of water stays the same, the form that this water takes does change—a lot!

20

JUST 4 LAUGHS!

How do you make water?
You need everything from H to O.

Earth's water moves through a **WATER CYCLE**, also known as the hydrologic cycle. This is Earth's way of recycling water. The water cycle has four major processes. These are **EVAPORATION**, **CONDENSATION**, **PRECIPITATION**, and collection.

Water continuously moves as it works its way through these four processes. The water cycle has no beginning and no end. This is why water is a **RENEWABLE RESOURCE**. The water will always go somewhere. We use water, and we cannot run out of it. But we cannot create more water than we already have.

Water works its way through each process at different speeds. For example, water spends only a short time in the air as rain or snow. But the water in lakes may take decades to cycle. Water in oceans, glaciers, and some **AQUIFERS** takes thousands of years to cycle. In an area with little or no precipitation, like a desert, it could take a million years! Here, water is almost **NON-RENEWABLE**. There's so little rainfall in a desert that once water is used up there, it's not easily replaced.

WORDS to know

WATER CYCLE: the natural recycling of water through evaporation, condensation, precipitation, and collection.

EVAPORATION: when a liquid heats up and changes to a gas.

CONDENSATION: when water vapor changes to liquid.

PRECIPITATION: falling moisture in the form of rain, sleet, snow, and hail.

RENEWABLE RESOURCE: a substance like water that goes through the same cycle again and again. It doesn't get used up.

AQUIFER: an underground layer of rock that has space in it that holds water.

NON-RENEWABLE: something you can run out of.

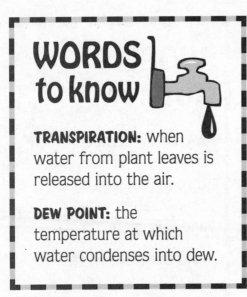

WORDS to know

TRANSPIRATION: when water from plant leaves is released into the air.

DEW POINT: the temperature at which water condenses into dew.

EVAPORATION

It's raining, it's pouring. And while the old man is snoring, puddles form all over the playground. At recess, the sun comes out, and the puddles start to disappear. The water just goes into the air.

The heat of the sun causes this to happen. When water changes from a liquid into a vapor it's called evaporation. Water evaporates at all temperatures. But heat really speeds along the process. Think about a tea kettle. When the water in the kettle is heated, it doesn't take long before the whistling sound tells you that the water is evaporating!

The water from oceans, seas, and lakes provide 90 percent of the water vapor in the atmosphere. Some water also moves into the air through the leaves of plants and trees. This process is called **TRANSPIRATION**. Once in the air, water vapor is spread throughout the atmosphere by the wind.

CONDENSATION

There's nothing like a cold glass of water on a hot day! But soon you notice that beads of water form on the outside of the glass. Is there a leak? No. What's happening is that the water vapor in the hot air is cooled when it touches the cold glass. The cold turns the water vapor back into liquid water. This is called condensation. It is the opposite of evaporation.

Meet A Scientist

Alfred Wegener (1880-1930) was a famous German meteorologist. He created the first balloons to track weather.

You can see condensation in your own backyard. On cool mornings, there is condensation on the grass. This is dew. Dew appears because the moisture in the air condenses as the air temperature falls overnight. The **DEW POINT** is the temperature at which water vapor condenses. The dew evaporates back into the air when the air temperature rises during the morning.

PRECIPITATION

Water that evaporates doesn't stay in the air for very long. It can only last for about 12 days, or less, before it becomes precipitation. Precipitation is any moisture that falls from the sky, such as rain, snow, sleet, or hail. Each day 241 trillion gallons (914 trillion liters) of precipitation falls on Earth. Less than 1 percent of Earth's water is in the air at one time. Three-quarters of all precipitation falls in the oceans. The rest falls on the land.

Mt. Waialeale in Hawaii is the wettest place on Earth, averaging over 451 inches of rainfall a year (1,145 centimeters). But Cherranpunji in India has the record for the most rainfall in a single year. In 1861 it rained 905 inches (2,297 centimeters)!

The water vapor that rises into the air doesn't become precipitation right away. First it becomes clouds. It's cooler up in the sky, so when water vapor rises it condenses into little ice crystals that bump and stick together. These are clouds.

The clouds keep growing, getting heavier, until gravity starts pulling them down. They fall as rain. If the temperature is cold enough near the ground, snowflakes fall. Sometime falling snowflakes melt completely but freeze again just before the surface. This is freezing rain. It makes any surface as slippery as an ice rink.

WORDS to know

RUNOFF: water that flows off the land.

PERCOLATE: to soak through.

GROUNDWATER: underground water found in aquifers.

Unlike snow or freezing rain, hail can fall at any time of the year. Hail forms in thunderclouds. It happens when falling ice droplets hit a warm updraft of air. This sends the ice droplets back up into the cloud again, where more ice attaches to the droplets. This can happen again and again, until the hail is heavy enough to fall through the warm updraft.

Hail can be as big as a baseball. Hailstones can rip tree trunks in half, break windows, and even shatter roofs! The largest hailstone in the United States fell in 2010 in Vivian, South Dakota. It weighed nearly 2 pounds (907 grams).

X-TREME PLANTS

Plants are amazing. They live in the most extreme places. There are plants on high mountain peaks and in the deep chilly depths of the ocean. There are even plants on a 1,242-mile (2,000-kilometer) strip of desert in Peru and Chile where it hasn't rained in thousands of years! In order to survive, the Huarango tree traps fog from the Pacific Ocean on its leaves. The leaves absorb the water, which travels to the roots. These roots can grow to over 200 feet long! Because they are so long, the roots reach water buried deep below the ground.

COLLECTION

Where does water collect before it starts evaporating again? Most water goes into the ocean. This isn't surprising since oceans cover over 70 percent of the earth. Water also flows over land into lakes, rivers, and streams as **RUNOFF**. Some precipitation soaks or **PERCOLATES** into the ground, where it becomes **GROUNDWATER**. This is one source of our drinking water. There is enough water under the ground that if it were to spread all over the earth's surface, it would be 180 feet thick (55 meters)!

The American Pioneers had to fetch water from a creek, river, or well and carry it back to their homes in buckets. Today, we just turn on a tap!

WORDS to know

UNSATURATED ZONE: an underground area that contains soil and air.

SATURATED ZONE: an underground area filled with water.

WATER TREATMENT PLANT: a place where water is cleaned.

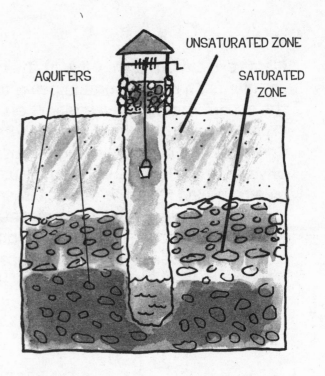

AQUIFERS

UNSATURATED ZONE

SATURATED ZONE

When water first enters the soil it encounters the **UNSATURATED ZONE**. This area is full of dirt and air. Some of the water that collects here is used by plants. The rest of the water goes deeper, into the **SATURATED ZONE**, which is filled with water. Here the water collects in cracks between rocks called aquifers. This water will begin a very slow journey through the ground to the ocean. Eventually, all collected water will evaporate and begin the water cycle again.

Meet A Scientist

William Morris Davis (1850–1934) was an American meteorologist. He showed how rivers create landforms through erosion.

CLOUDY WITH A CHANCE OF HAMBURGER BUNS

What do raindrops look like? Do they have pointy tops and round bottoms? No! They actually look like hamburger buns and beans. The smallest raindrops, less than 0.01 inch across (1 millimeter), are round spheres. Medium-sized raindrops, about 0.12 inches (3 millimeters), look like beans. Anything over 0.2 inches (4.5 millimeters) resembles a hamburger bun. That's pretty cool!

Next time it rains, catch raindrops and measure their size. Just spread a thin layer of baking grease on a cookie sheet and catch a few raindrops on it. The raindrops will make holes in the grease. Now you can measure a raindrop's width.

THEN+NOW

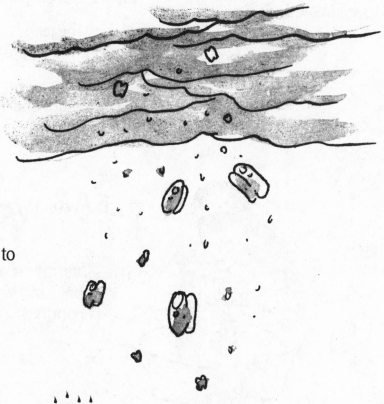

THEN: In ancient Egypt, the Egyptians put water from the Nile River into large jars. They waited for the mud to settle. Then they drank only the water from the top.

NOW: Today, towns and cities have **WATER TREATMENT PLANTS** to kill dangerous bacteria in drinking water.

Bell Jar Terrarium

You can watch the water cycle at work in a terrarium. This is a miniature garden in a jar. The jar traps the water vapor given off by the plants. The water condenses and runs down the sides of the jar back to the soil. This keeps the soil moist for your plant.

Supplies

large glass food jar with a lid

soil

small rocks

moss

small seeds or plants

twigs

1 Clean and dry your jar and lid. Put soil, small rocks, and wet moss on the lid. Add small plants or seeds, and twigs.

2 Screw the jar onto the lid. The jar will be upside down.

3 Place your tiny ecosystem in a sunny spot and enjoy!

CLEAN WATER TECH

The Lifestraw is a portable water filter. It kills bacteria when a person drinks water through it.

Transpiration Experiment

Water helps plants grow. The water travels from the roots of the plant through the stem to the leaves. Some of the water in the plant's leaves evaporates into the air. This is transpiration.

1 Place a plastic bag over each plant and fasten securely with a twist tie.

2 Place the plants in a sunny place.

3 The following day, check the plants.

Things to Notice

≈ **How long did it take for water to collect in the bags?**

≈ **Do the bags have the same amount of water? Why do you think this is?**

≈ **Would your results change if you placed the plants in a dark place?**

JUST 4 LAUGHS!

What did April bring her friend May?
Flowers!

29

Water Cycle Wrist Band

**The water cycle is all around you.
Now you can even wear it on your wrist!**

1 Cut the foot and top off a sock. Fold the top and bottom edges of the middle section down and inside ½ inch (1 centimeter). Secure the edges with fabric glue.

2 Divide the sock bracelet vertically into four sections. Each section represents a process in the water cycle.

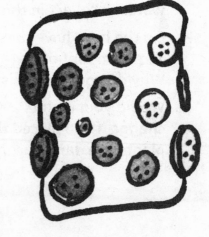

3 Sew or glue the beads and buttons into each section in the following order:

≋ **white for evaporation**

≋ **yellow for condensation**

≋ **light blue for precipitation**

≋ **dark blue for collection**

4 If you used glue, let the bracelet dry before wearing.

5 Make another for a friend.

WATER AND WEATHER

MANY PEOPLE CHECK THE WEATHER WHEN THEY GET UP IN THE MORNING. With a click of their computer mouse, the local weather map lights up the computer screen. Knowing the weather makes it easier to plan activities. It's also easier to choose our clothing when we know what the temperature is going to be.

It might seem that weather is created right outside your door, but it isn't. It takes place in the atmosphere. The atmosphere is a blanket of gases around the earth. It receives energy from the sun. This energy creates the weather. Weather is the wind, heavy rain, snow flurries, clouds, or sun you get each day.

What is climate? Climate describes patterns of weather over a period of years. Some people live in rainy climates, others live in hot and dry climates. **Climate is controlled by:**

* ✳ Earth's rotation
* ✳ Earth's movement around the sun
* ✳ Earth's atmosphere
* ✳ Oceans and their currents

WORDS to know

HUMIDITY: the amount of moisture in the air.

HUMIDITY

It is a warm day. The clothes line is full of laundry. Will it dry? It depends on how much **HUMIDITY** there is. Humidity is the amount of moisture in the air. It changes all the time. High humidity is when there is a lot of water in the air. Your skin feels sticky. Low humidity is when there is little moisture in the air. Your skin is cool to touch. The laundry on the clothes line will dry much quicker when the humidity is low.

LOW HUMIDITY = DRY AIR

HIGH HUMIDITY = WET AIR

CLOUDS

Lying in the grass you watch the clouds change shape. That one looks like a fluffy bunny! And there's a castle! No matter what they look like, clouds all have the same basic ingredients.

It begins with water. All water eventually evaporates due to the heat of the planet's surface. The water becomes a gas—water vapor. Heat rises, so up the water vapor goes, high into the sky.

The biggest ice cubes in the world are icebergs. In 2010 an iceberg 925 square miles in size (2,500 square kilometers) broke off from Antarctica. That's about as big as Rhode Island.

The higher it goes, the colder it gets. The cold makes the water vapor change back into a solid—water droplets. Water droplets are super tiny and unbelievably light—so light that they can float in the air. But water droplets don't hang out by themselves for long. They're "sticky." So they gather together with other droplets. The result is a cloud.

Clouds are important. They create precipitation like rain and snow. They also help to warm the earth. That's because clouds absorb the sun's heat during the day. Then they spread that heat out in all directions. So if you want to stay warm when roasting marshmallows outside, choose a cloudy night over a clear one.

Meet A Scientist

Pierre Perrault (1608–1680) was a French scientist. He showed that rain feeds springs and rivers.

NAME THAT CLOUD

People have gazed at the clouds for many thousands of years. Artists have painted them. Poets have written about them. But there was no scientific way to describe clouds.

That changed in 1802, with Luke Howard. Luke loved science. Watching the weather was his hobby. He wrote a paper about his weather observations. At first he placed clouds into three major groups. Later he added a fourth. Each group had its own unique features. He gave Latin names to the most commonly seen clouds. We still use Luke Howard's system today.

CIRRUS

NIMBUS

CUMULUS

STRATUS

○ CIRRUS CLOUDS are thin and wispy. They are a sign of fair weather.

○ NIMBUS CLOUDS are dark gray. Watch out! They mean a storm is coming.

○ CUMULUS CLOUDS are fluffy like cotton candy. They usually mean fair weather, but they can also grow and create heavy showers, even tornadoes!

○ STRATUS CLOUDS blanket the sky like a gray sheet. They are a sign of changing weather.

WORDS to know

MIGRATION: when animals move from one area to another.

WEATHER FORECAST: to predict what the weather will be.

WEATHER TOOLS

For most of history, people have relied on their own two eyes to predict the weather. Native Americans watched animal **MIGRATIONS**. During the spring and fall months, animals moved in search of food, water, and shelter. Flowering plants marked the seasons. European settlers in America created their weather traditions from their own observations. These passed down as sayings like, "Clear moon, frost soon." Sayings are easy to remember. But they are not fact. So they are not always reliable.

The invention of weather tools made it possible to measure the weather. The barometer measures pressure in the atmosphere. The anemometer measures wind speed. When long-distance communication was made possible by the invention of the telegraph in the 1840s, weather stations were set up across America. It was now possible to track weather systems. This was the beginning of weather maps and **WEATHER FORECASTS**.

What do meteorologists do? The scientific study of the weather is called meteorology. A person who studies the weather is called a meteorologist. **Meteorologists**:

* **collect** satellite and other weather data.

* **observe** the atmosphere and notice if weather patterns change or stay the same.

* **organize** their data on computers. They use this data to predict storms and better understand global warming and climate change.

THUNDERSTORMS

You don't have the technology to track thunderstorms. But a simple method will tell you how close a thunderstorm is to you. When you see a lightning flash, start counting the seconds. Stop when you hear the thunder. Divide the number of seconds by five. That's how many miles the thunderstorm is from you. If you divide by three, you'll get kilometers. Light travels much faster than sound, so you see the lightning long before you hear the thunder.

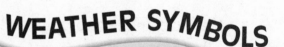

WEATHER SYMBOLS

Meteorologists do not have to use words to describe the weather. They can use symbols. Use the weather element list below to create your own weather symbols.

◊ Drizzle	◊ Snow	◊ Fog
◊ Rain	◊ Thunder	◊ Freezing rain

Meteorologist Journal

Supplies

10 to 15 sheets of found paper

ruler

pencil

scissors

pencil crayons

hole punch

2 metal D rings

Record your weather observations in your very own journal. This journal is earth friendly. It uses recycled paper such as old graph paper, used envelopes, and other scraps.

1 Stack paper and decide on a journal size.

2 Using a ruler, pencil, and scissors, cut the random sheets into the same size.

3 Choose one piece for your cover and decorate it to your liking.

4 Punch holes at the top and bottom of the spine. Insert D rings into the holes.

5 Every day, record what you see. How warm is it when you get up each morning? Is it snowy, wind? What do the clouds look like? Can you start to see patterns in the weather?

MY METEOROLOGIST JOURNAL

JUST 4 LAUGHS!

Why didn't thunder go first? **Because thunder always follows lightning.**

Hair Hygrometer

Supplies

plastic folder

scissors

ruler

a strand of hair

tape

cardboard

tack

marker

hair dryer

In 1783 scientists created a tool called a hair hygrometer. This measured changes in humidity using a single strand of hair. They had realized that hair changes with the humidity.

1 From the plastic folder cut out an arrow pointer 1.5 inches wide by 7 inches long (4 by 18 centimeters).

2 Tape one end of the hair to the flat end of the pointer, 1 inch (2 centimeters) in from the edge. Tape the other end of the hair to the top of the cardboard so it hangs down.

3 Attach the pointer to cardboard with a tack, ½ inch (1 centimeter) in from the edge. The tack should fit loosely so the pointer pivots.

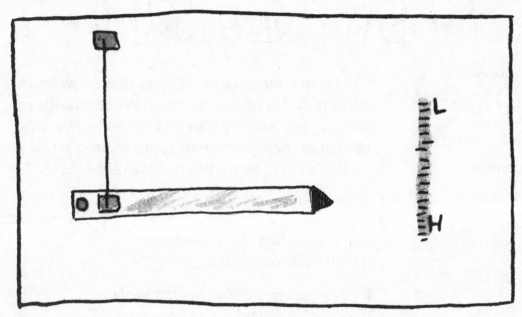

4. Draw a 4-inch (10-centimeter) scale so that the pointer lines up with the 1-inch mark (2-centimeter).

5. With a hair dryer set on low, blow air on the hair for a few seconds and watch what happens.

6. Next, bring your hygrometer into a steamy bathroom. Does the pointer move? Hair is made of a protein called keratin. The bonds that hold this protein together break down when there is water, making hair stretch. When there is high humidity the hair lengthens and the pointer moves down. When there is low humidity the hair shortens and the pointer moves up.

Things to Notice

≈ **Did the air feel different when the humidity changed?**

≈ **Make hygrometers with hair from different family members. Do you think the results will be different?**

Snowflake Slides

Supplies

- black paper
- silver glitter pen
- 2 plastic microscope slides or acetate
- plastic juice ring
- metallic tape
- scissors
- cord or string

"Under the microscope, I found that snowflakes were miracles of beauty," said Wilson Bentley (1885–1931). Bentley was a Vermont farmer who photographed more than 5,000 snow crystals. Here's a way to make your own snowflake.

1 Draw a snowflake on black paper with a silver glitter pen. It must be small enough to fit between two microscope slides.

2 Place your design between two plastic microscope slides. Or fashion your own slides from acetate.

3 Glue the juice container ring to one edge of the slides or acetate.

4 Wrap the edges of the slide or acetate together with metallic tape.

5 Attach the string to the ring and hang your snowflake up. Or make the cord longer and wear it as a necklace.

THEN+NOW

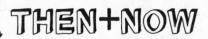

THEN: Ancient cultures, such as the Greeks, believed weather was controlled by the Gods.

NOW: Today, we know that weather happens in the atmosphere. It is caused by the sun and the water cycle.

Nilometer

In Ancient Egypt, the Nile River was the main source of water. Every year the river would flood. The Egyptians needed to know if the flood was going to be light, normal, or heavy. So they built a nilometer. A nilometer is basically a staircase leading down to the river. The stairs had measurements written on them. The Egyptians would then observe how far up the steps the water rose to. In this activity you are going to make a fun variation of a nilometer to measure rainfall.

Supplies

6 plastic bottle caps, each 1½ inches high (4 centimeters)

water-soluble glue

permanent marker

ruler

plastic container

waterproof marker

scissors

fishing wire

1. Glue the bottle caps to form a staircase. Staggering them as shown in the picture.

2. When the glue is dry, use a marker to make marks every quarter inch (½ centimeter) on each cap.

3. Glue the base of the staircase to the bottom of the container.

4. With scissors, make two holes in the top of the container, one on each side.

5. Thread fishing wire through the holes and secure the container to a fence.

6. After each rainfall check the level of the water. Record your measurements in your meteorologist's journal. Then empty you nilometer so it's ready for the next rain storm.

41

WATER WORKS

WHEN YOU THINK OF AMAZING INVENTIONS, YOU PROBABLY THINK OF A JET PLANE OR A ROBOT. But how about a simple drain? Every day you flush a toilet or turn on a faucet. Not so long ago these simple actions would have been impossible.

Since ancient times, people have wanted to control water. A good source of freshwater could help build a great civilization, like Egypt, Rome, or Greece. Too much uncontrolled water could cause destruction. And too little water could turn the land to dust. So people invented tools and structures that could hold water, move water, and lift water.

FROM HERE TO THERE

Water is always on the move, but it doesn't always go where you want it to go. To control the flow of water, ancient people had to build elaborate systems. People in the Middle East and North Africa, for example, built **IRRIGATION** tunnels called **QUANATS**. These guided water from faraway mountain streams into villages. One quanat in Iran stretched over 25 miles (40 kilometers).

The Romans built structures above and below ground to control the flow of water. **AQUEDUCTS** were enormous stone structures that bridged valleys and rivers to bring water to Rome. Some brought water from as far away as 57 miles (92 kilometers). Some Roman aqueducts are still in use today!

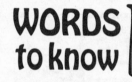

WORDS to know

IRRIGATION: transporting water through canals or tunnels to water **CROPS**.

CROP: a plant grown for food or other uses.

QUANAT: an underground water tunnel.

AQUEDUCT: a network of channels used to direct water over long distances.

CISTERN: an underground well used for storing water.

All this water couldn't be used at once. It had to be stored in huge underground wells, called **CISTERNS**. Some cisterns, like the Basilica Cistern in Turkey, are breathtaking. Built in 532 CE, it is so big that a small boat can row between the 336 marble pillars.

THE SHADUF

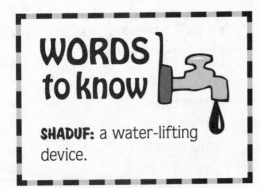

Ancient Egyptians used the Nile River for their source of water. When the Nile flooded every year, it left behind rich soil that was good for growing crops. But when the flood waters left, the farmland dried up. So the ancient Egyptians invented the **SHADUF** to water their crops.

The shaduf lifts water from the river with a long beam that rests on a stand. It's like a giant seesaw. When one end goes up, the other goes down. On one end is a large bucket and on the other end is a heavy stone.

First the farmer pulls the bucket down into the river. Then the farmer goes to the other end of the shaduf and pulls down on the stone. This lifts the water-filled bucket out of the river. The farmer then swings the bucket around and pours the water into a canal. Water in the canal flows to the farmland. This system works so well that farmers around the world still use the shaduf to water their crops!

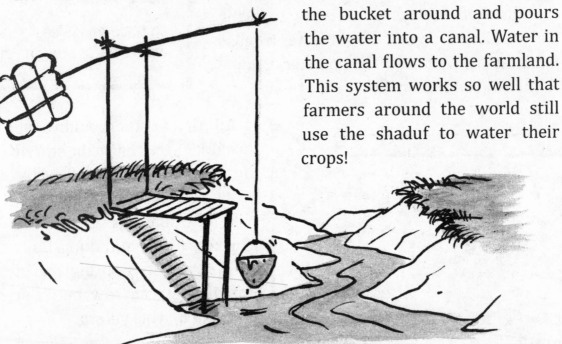

SUSTAINABLE WATER POWER

Energy sources that last forever are considered renewable. Wind power is renewable. So is energy from the sun. You can't run out of it. Renewable energy is also called green power and clean energy because it does not produce **POLLUTION**.

WORDS to know

POLLUTION: man-made waste that dirties an environment.

GEOTHERMAL: a form of heat energy from the earth's core.

GEOTHERMAL energy is another kind of renewable energy. It comes from underground water that is warmed by heat from the earth's core. The earth's core is always producing heat. The word geothermal comes from two Greek words: *geo* means earth and *therme* means heat.

Almost 90 percent of all homes in Iceland are heated by geothermal energy. Iceland is the perfect place for using geothermal energy because it has the greatest number of active volcanoes in the world.

Moving water can produce a lot of energy. It can wash away soil during storms and floods. It can even, over thousands of years, carve away at huge cliffs. This erosion creates amazing natural wonders, like the Grand Canyon!

THEN+NOW

THEN: In ancient Rome 2,000 years ago, fires were hard to put out. Hundreds of Roman men passed water buckets hand-to-hand to fight fire.

NOW: Today, cities and towns have fire stations with trained people. They use trucks that store tons of water, and pumps that blast water into fires.

WORDS to know

WATER WHEEL: a wheel with paddles attached that spins when water flows over it. The energy can be used to power machines or lift water.

WATER WHEELS

WATER WHEELS capture the renewable energy of moving water. A large framework supports an axle on which the wheel sits. Dams funnel water towards the wheel. The water wheel spins freely as water pushes it.

Some water wheels are placed directly in a fast flowing stream. This style of wheel turns as the current hits the paddles. Other water wheels need water to rush over their top. The weight of the water forces the wheel to turn. The wheel can be attached to machines. In the past, water wheels moved heavy stones inside mills to grind grain.

No one knows who invented the water wheel. There are many variations around the world. Some are horizontal, while others are vertical. The ancient Greeks and Romans left records of their designs. But the Chinese may have used water wheels centuries earlier.

Each summer Alaskan glaciers melt. This melt provides 50,000 billion gallons (189 kiloliters) of moving water.

46

WORDS to know

HYDROELECTRICITY: electricity created from falling water.

TURBINE: a machine with rotating blades that changes one type of energy into another.

At one point in Chinese history, over 200 water wheels stood along the banks of the Yellow River in the city of Lanzhou. It's no wonder Lanzhou was called the capital of the water wheel! Some of the largest wheels were 49 to 59 feet high (15 to 18 meters).

HYDROPOWER

Hydropower is energy produced by falling water. Some of the electricity we use comes from hydropower. In fact, the United States is one of the largest producers of **HYDROELECTRICITY** in the world. One of the most spectacular sources of hydropower is Niagara Falls in New York. Every second, 150, 000 gallons (568 kiloliters) of water crash over Niagara Falls. In 1895, an inventor named Nikola Tesla built a hydroelectric plant at Niagara Falls. It transfers electricity over long distances. Niagara Falls is still the largest producer of electricity in the state of New York.

How does electricity come from falling water?

* Falling water forces a **TURBINE** to spin.

* The spinning turbine powers a generator. This makes electricity.

* Electricity travels through lines to your home.

What kind of fish are educated? **A school of fish.**

THREE GORGES DAM

Hydroelectricity doesn't just come from waterfalls. It also comes from rivers. But first a dam has to be built. Dams are giant structures that stop the flow of a river. This creates a large lake behind the dam wall. As water from the lake is released through the dam wall it spins the turbines. This creates electricity.

The world's largest dam is the Three Gorges Dam in China. It is nearly

600 feet high (183 meters), with a reservoir almost 400 miles long (644 kilometers)! Its 26 generators produce 18,000 megawatts of electricity for millions of Chinese people. When the dam was built, the huge lake destroyed 19 cities, 300 villages, and many important sites left by ancient people. Nearly two million people had to move.

Meet A Scientist

Ben Franklin (1706–1790) recorded weather patterns. He tried to figure out what caused different weather conditions. He was one of the first people to realize that storms can move against the direction of the wind.

WAVE & TIDAL ENERGY

Energy can also come from the ocean. As the wind blows across the water, it creates waves. Waves are a source of energy, but it's not easy to harness this energy. Equipment must be able to stand up to rough seas.

Imagine huge red tubes the size of railroad cars floating out in the ocean. This is not a sea monster hoax, but a modern wave power station. The waves move joints connecting the tubes, which power an electrical generator. The first wave-powered farm in America is under construction off the coast of Oregon.

Tides are also a source of energy. One of the largest tidal plants in the world is in the Bay of Fundy in Canada. The plant captures some of the power from the 100 billion tons of water that flow into and out of the bay each day. That is more water than all the freshwater river flows in the world! Currently the plant supplies about 6,000 homes with energy. Eventually, it should supply enough energy for 100,000 homes.

CLEAN WATER TECH

In the future, a nanosponge might provide clean water in poor countries. Fitted to taps, the sponge catches dirt in its tiny holes as water pours through.

Archimedes Screw

The Archimedes screw is a 2,000-year-old invention. It was invented by the Greek scientist who also discovered why some things can float. The Archimedes screw is used to transfer low-lying water up into irrigation canals.

Supplies

straw

pipe cleaner

acetate or clear plastic folder

tape

2 bowls

sugar

1. Poke one end of the pipe cleaner through the straw to secure it.

2. Wind the pipe cleaner around the straw to make the screw. Make certain that the space between the spirals is even.

3. Tightly wrap a piece of acetate around the screw to make a cylinder. Secure it with tape. It should fit snuggly, but the screw should still be able to turn.

4. Pour sugar into a bowl and insert your screw at an angle. Turn the screw, not the cylinder, and watch as the sugar moves up. You can pour this sugar into a second bowl. Use your Archimedes screw to move all of the sugar from one bowl to another.

Things to Notice

≈ As the rod turns, what happens to the lowest point and highest point of the spiral?

≈ How is the sugar pulled along?

Make a Shaduf

Ancient Egyptians used the shaduf to lift water. Here is a fun way to make your own.

1. Position the middle of the long stick in the V of the other stick, like a seesaw. Secure it with yarn and set it to one side.

2. Make 2 holes on opposite sides at the top edge of the plastic cup. Thread yarn through the holes leaving a long loop to hang it on the stick. Tie it off at each hole.

3. Tie the cup to one end of the long stick. There should be enough yarn to adjust the length so the cup can reach the water source.

4. Tie another piece of yarn around the stone. Attach it to the other end of the stick. Leave enough length so that you can move the stone up and down the stick to balance the water.

5. Securely place the V stick in the ground near a water source. Try to collect water. If you need to, make adjustments to the length of the yarn or to its placement on the stick.

Things to Notice

≈ **Does the weight of the cup change your experiment?**

≈ **How does the length of the straight stick affect your shaduf?**

≈ **What was the hardest thing about building the shaduf?**

Mini Water Wheel

Supplies

plastic lid

scissors

waterproof markers

ruler

hot glue gun

spool

acetate or recycled plastic folder

straw

The water wheel was important to Colonial American life. Before electricity, the colonists needed the mill to grind grains like wheat, corn, and oats.

1 Cut out a circle 3 inches in diameter from a plastic lid (8 centimeters). Use waterproof markers to decorate the top of the circle.

2 On the underside, divide the circle into 6 even sections. Have an adult help you poke a hole through the center.

3 With an adult, hot glue a spool to the underside of circle. Be careful not to glue the hole.

4 From the acetate or recycled plastic folder, cut out 6 tabs for paddles. They should measure 1 inch by 1½ inches (1 by 4 centimeters).

5 Bend the tabs slightly at the bottom. Hot glue them to the underside of the circle around the spool. Space them out evenly.

6 Push the straw through the spool and circle. It has to move freely. The straw is the axle. Center your wheel on the straw. Now hold it under running water and see what happens.

Things to Notice

≋ Does your wheel spin faster when it is nearer the water source or farther away?

≋ How much water do you need to make the wheel turn?

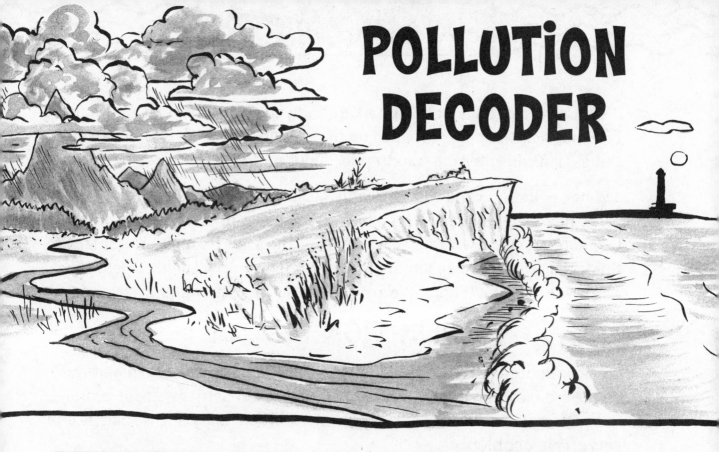

POLLUTION DECODER

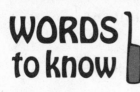

WATERSHED: an area that drains into a **WATERWAY**.

WATERWAY: a channel of water such as a stream or river.

AFTER RAIN FALLS FROM THE SKY, IT FLOWS INTO LOW AREAS OF LAND. This land then drains into a body of water, such as a pond, reservoir, or ocean. The rivers, lakes, and land on which water runs off is a **WATERSHED**.

No matter where you live, you are in a watershed. Your actions can help keep the water in your part of the watershed clean. Or it can add to the pollution.

You cannot miss pollution. It's all around you. Soap from washing your bike, popsicle wrappers dropped on the ground, and Rover's poop are all things that can enter the water cycle. Pollutants make water dirty.

Water pollution can even be deadly. According to the United Nations, every day 2 million tons of human waste ends up in Earth's waterways. Untreated factory waste also ends up in the water supply. You might think that what happens in another town or country couldn't possibly affect your life, but it does. We are all part of the same water cycle.

POLLUTION PUZZLE

After a raindrop falls from the sky, it can come into contact with pollution on the ground. Water pollution has many causes. Whether we're at home, in town, at work, or on the farm, we make water dirty. How can we solve this problem?

* Litter left behind can pollute a beach, park, or campsite.
  Clean up after yourself.

* Lawn chemicals harm fish and plants that live in the water.
  Pull weeds out instead of using chemicals.

* Pet poop spreads harmful bacteria.
  Put it in the trash.

* Dirt running into rivers makes them warm and cloudy.
  Sweep dirt into the garden.

WORDS to know

BIODEGRADABLE: can be broken down by nature.

NON-BIODEGRADABLE: cannot be broken down by nature.

PHOSPHORUS: a chemical.

WASTEWATER

In your home, what does wastewater sound like? It sounds like a flush, a swish, or a whoosh. Whatever goes down the drain is wastewater. But not all waste is the same. Some waste breaks down in nature. It is **BIODEGRADABLE**. It was once part of a living thing. Other waste does not break down. It is **NON-BIODEGRADABLE**. It was never part of any living thing.

Some soaps, shampoos, and cleaning products contain **PHOSPHORUS**. When this chemical gets in the water, it makes some plants, like algae, grow like crazy. Algae is that slimy green stuff you sometimes see in water. When algae dies and rots, it uses up a lot of the oxygen in the water. Too much rotting algae uses up all the oxygen, so fish and other living creatures cannot live in the water.

You can make a difference. Look for the biodegradable symbol on the things you buy. It tells you if a product is biodegradable. There are biodegradable cleaning products, plastics, and furniture. There are even biodegradable knives and forks made from corn!

BIODEGRADABLE?

Do you know what is biodegradable and what is non-biodegradable?

A. Hair   C. Toilet Paper

B. Dental Floss   D. Soap

Answers: A/B, B/NB, C/B, D/NB

Biodegradable Symbol

WASTE WATER ADVENTURE WITH SUPER WATER

This is Super Water. Watch it dive into the drain. See it slip down the pipe joining your home to the town's sewer. Here our hero meets with more water molecules plus pollution, toilet paper, food scraps, and poop. Oh no, here comes the dreaded FOG—fat, oil, and grease. Downhill by gravity, to the treatment plant they go. A screen at the plant catches large trash like sticks or toys. Super Water sails on through. Next is the grit chamber. Sand and gravel sink to the bottom. Machines skim fat, oil, and grease off the top. A dose of chlorine or ultraviolet light kills off bacteria. Yeah! Super Water is free to flow into a waterway. It is part of the water cycle all over again.

Try making your own water adventure comic.

ACID RAIN

WORDS to know

SULFUR DIOXIDE: a colorless gas or liquid that adds to air pollution and acid rain.

NITROGEN OXIDE: a colorless gas or liquid that adds to air pollution and acid rain.

PH SCALE: a scale that measures acids.

Who put the acid in acid rain? We did. When we burn fossil fuels like coal, gasoline, or oil for energy, we create **SULFUR DIOXIDE** and **NITROGEN OXIDE**. These gases make the water vapor in the air more acidic. When this water vapor turns into rain, you've got acid rain. Actually, any form of precipitation such as snow, sleet, hail, or even fog can be acid rain.

You can measure the amount of acid in acid rain with the **PH SCALE**. A zero on the scale is the most acidic and 14.0 is the least acidic. Any reading of 5.5 or above is considered clean. Anything below 5.5 is acid rain.

Just how harmful is acid rain? There are thousands of lakes around the world that are crystal clear and beautiful. But they are dead. They contain no living creatures or plants. This is from years of acid rain. It changed the chemical balance in the soil around these lakes. When the soil couldn't absorb the acid from the rain any longer, it flowed into the lakes.

Meet A Scientist

Edmond Halley (1656–1742) was a scientist and astronomer who also studied hydrology. He proved that water that evaporates from waterways comes down as precipitation.

CLOACA MAXIMA

Human waste is not a new problem. People have always dealt with it. Sometimes it went into rivers. More often than not, it went on the street. Yuck! This still happens in some places in the world today.

The Romans invented the first sewer, called the Cloaca Maxima, 2,500 years ago. Parts of it were big enough for a horse and cart to drive through! At first the Cloaca Maxima drained swampy land around Rome. The swamps were a source of insects and disease. Later, it drained dirty water from the city. There were no water treatment plants, so the sewage ran straight into the Tiber River in Rome. The sewer worked for 2,000 years.

Acid rain affects everything. It damages statues, buildings, and pipes. The acid reacts with the building materials and softens them. Every time it rains, monuments like the Coliseum in Italy or the Statue of Liberty in New York City are in danger. Some monuments and buildings are badly damaged—worn smooth by acid rain.

The news is not good but that doesn't mean that people should just give up. No way! Some solutions require governments to work together. Others are simple steps you can take. What small changes can you make to the way you live that can have a big impact?

* Use public transportation.

* Only run a full dishwasher.

* Air dry your laundry.

* Walk or bike instead of travelling by car.

* Turn off the lights when you leave a room.

FLOATING GARBAGE

Litter causes big problems. And when it comes to litter in the world's oceans, those problems are enormous. In the Pacific Ocean, for example, there's an area called the "Garbage Patch." This area contains millions of pounds of garbage. Some scientists believe it to be twice as big as the state of Texas!

Lake Baikal in Russia is the largest freshwater lake in the world. It contains one fifth of the world's freshwater.

The United Nations estimates that every square mile of ocean contains 46,000 pieces of floating plastic. Some of this garbage sinks to the ocean floor, where it harms fish and aquatic plants. It may even wash up on a shore near you.

LITTER LIFE SPAN

Have you ever wondered how long it takes for littler to break down? It all depends on the litter . . .

TYPE OF LITTER	TIME TO BREAK DOWN
Cardboard	2 weeks
Foam	50 years
Aluminum	200 years
Plastic packaging	400 years
Glass	1 million years
Styrofoam	Never!

WORDS to know

PRECYCLE: reducing waste by purchasing a product with less packaging—or not buying it at all.

CRUDE OIL: thick, natural oil.

A great way to reduce litter is to **PRECYCLE**. THINK if you really need an item before you buy it. If you do need it, choose one with less packaging. When shopping, bring your own bag. It just takes too many weeks and years for litter to break down.

OIL SPILL

We see it all too often on the news—a dark, thick sheen stretching for miles over the ocean. This is the signature of a **CRUDE OIL** spill. In 1989, thousands of animals died when an oil tanker called the *Exxon Valdez* spilled near Alaska. As many as 350,000 sea otters died. More recently, in 2010, a BP oil pipe burst into the Gulf of Mexico. It harmed many animals, including bluefin tuna, dolphins, and sharks. We only hear about large spills like these, but oil pollutes the oceans every day. Each year, over 300,000 sea birds die off the Atlantic Coast from illegal oil dumping.

JUST 4 LAUGHS!

Why do weather men carry dog biscuits and cat nip?
In case it rains cats and dogs.

Oil spills are not easy to clean up. Oil does not dissolve in water. Instead, it forms a thick sludge. Fish suffocate in it. The feathers of birds absorb it, making them unable to fly. If a bird tries to clean the oil off its feathers, it only poisons itself. Plants and animals along the shore are also at risk.

THEN+NOW

THEN: In the past, water pipes were made of lead, terracotta, clay, or wood—such as bamboo.

NOW: Today, water pipes are made of plastic, steel, and cast-iron.

CLEAN WATER ACT

Imagine paddling a canoe. The river is oily and slimy. Cans and plastic bags float in the water. Before 1972 there were many polluted waterways in the United States. There were no federal laws protecting them. Then the U.S. Congress passed the Clean Water Act to protect our rivers, lakes, and streams.

Water in Rome

Supplies

- scissors
- paper
- pencil
- poster board
- glue
- markers
- 2 to 3 players
- coins
- die

Julius Frontinus was one of Rome's most famous engineers. In this board game, help him fix Rome's water system.

1. Cut out 20 squares from the paper. Write one of the phrases listed here on one side of each square. Include the corresponding letter.

2. After filling in the squares, arrange them in a pattern in alphabetical order on the poster board. Glue each square in place. Decorate the rest of your gameboard with the markers.

A Hired!

B You are head of the Roman water supply.

C Fix the Cloaca Maxima, move ahead two squares.

D Write a report to the emperor, roll again.

E Robbed, move back to start.

F Build a public bath, move ahead one.

G Fix terracotta pipes.

H Public bath breaks, miss a turn.

I Workers happy, move ahead one.

J Water system mapped, go to end.

K Leaks in the system fixed.

L Fall while riding through aqueduct, miss a turn.

M Visit the Emperor.

N Day of rest.

O Water is stolen, go back three spaces.

P Check all systems, move ahead one square.

Q An aqueduct is tapped, miss a turn.

R Public fountains run, roll again.

S The emperor is pleased.

T Rome has water!

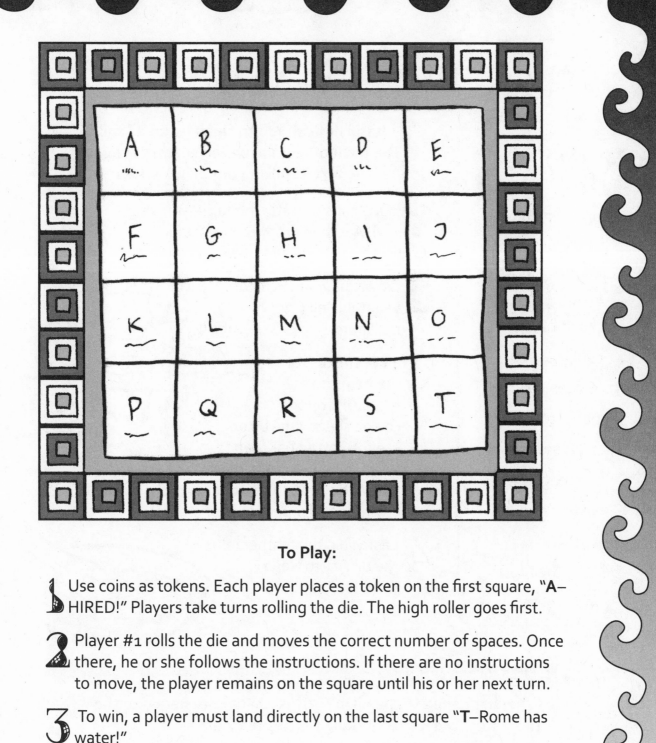

To Play:

1 Use coins as tokens. Each player places a token on the first square, "**A–HIRED!**" Players take turns rolling the die. The high roller goes first.

2 Player #1 rolls the die and moves the correct number of spaces. Once there, he or she follows the instructions. If there are no instructions to move, the player remains on the square until his or her next turn.

3 To win, a player must land directly on the last square "**T**–Rome has water!"

Oil Spill Experiment

Supplies

clear mixing bowl

water

blue food dye

½ cup vegetable oil (120 milliliters)

cookie sheet

cotton ball

paper towel

string

sponge

plastic bag

spoon

feather

detergent

It is a difficult job to clean up an oil spill. The oil floats on the water. Just try cleaning up an oil spill in your own kitchen!

1. Pour 2 cups of water into a clear mixing bowl. Add two drops of blue food dye to your ocean in a bowl.

2. Slowly pour in ½ cup of vegetable oil (120 milliliters).

3. Place the rest of the items on the supply list on the cookie sheet. One by one, use the cotton ball, paper towel, string, sponge, plastic bag, and spoon to try to remove the oil. Write down what happens in your journal.

4. Lastly, dip the feather in the oil. Try to clean it with detergent.

Things to Notice

≈ **What happened to the oil in the water? Did it sink or float or mix in?**

≈ **How much oil did each item soak up?**

≈ **What happened to the feather?**

≈ **Can you think of other ways to collect oil?**

Watershed Journey

In this activity, see what a water droplet picks up as it travels through the watershed. You will be working with food, so wash your hands before you begin and ask an adult for permission.

1 Measure and mix the first three ingredients in a bowl. Use all of the mixture to form bite-sized balls and set aside. These are your raindrops.

2 Place one topping on each plate. The muesli is for leaves, the chocolate sprinkles are for soil, the coconut is for lawn chemicals, the raisins are for detergents. Roll your "raindrops" through the toppings, one by one.

MUESLI   **SPRINKLES**   **COCONUT**   **RAISINS**

3 When your are finished rolling the contents of the bowl, share with friends.

Things to Notice

≈ **Where are the watersheds in your area?**

≈ **What are some ways you can keep your watersheds clean?**

≈ **Where does the water in your watershed eventually end up?**

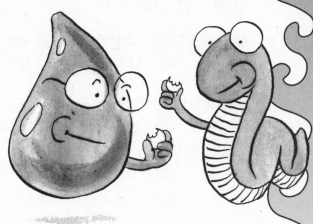

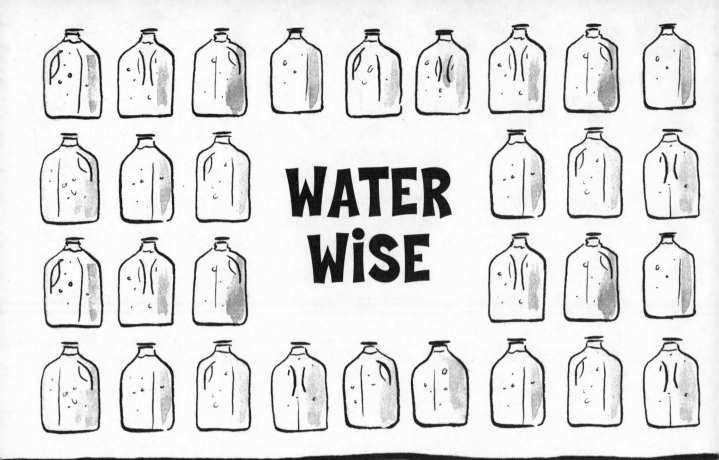

WATER WiSE

DRIP...DRIP...DRIP. A leaky tap can waste 24 gallons (90 liters) of water in one day. It is easy to see why every drop counts. When you brushed your teeth this morning, was the tap running? If so, millions of water molecules went down the drain.

Remember what we learned about water treatment plants? Every drop of water that goes down a drain is treated. This costs money and uses energy. It may seem like just a twist of the tap here and a flush there. But it adds up to a lot of water every day around the world. Just imagine how much it is in a week or a year!

HOW MUCH WATER DO YOU USE?

ACTIVITY	WATER USAGE
Toilet (each flush)	3 gallons (11 liters)
Average bath	50 gallons (190 liters)
Brushing teeth (1 time)	1 gallon (4 liters)
Laundry (1 load)	40 gallons (151 liters)

WORDS to know

DROUGHT: a long period of time without rain.

CONSERVE: to use something carefully, so it isn't used up.

LET'S CONSERVE!

It's estimated that by the year 2050, one in four people will be living in a country with freshwater shortages. The water system in North America faces challenges too. Parts of the United States have plentiful water supplies, while others often experience **DROUGHT**. Population growth and climate change will affect the water supply as well.

When you need water, all you have to do is turn on a tap. It's as easy as breathing. But using water wisely now is one way to make sure there will be clean drinking water in the future. Even today, one billion people in the world do not have safe drinking water. In the Kenyan village of Kipsaraman in Africa, there is only one source of freshwater. It's a water tap with a padlock on it. While we don't put locks on our taps, there are lots of ways we can **CONSERVE** water.

What can you do to conserve water?

* Turn off the tap when brushing your teeth.

* Keep a jug of water in the fridge instead of running the tap.

* Wash fruits and vegetables in a sink of water.

* Use a bucket of water, not the hose, to wash your bike.

REUSE WATER

WORDS to know

GRAYWATER: water that has been used for things like laundry or washing dishes.

XERISCAPING: gardening with native plants and less water.

Reusing **GRAYWATER** is another way to conserve water. This is water that results from washing dishes and clothes. The average person in the United States produces 150 gallons (568 liters) of graywater a day. Graywater contains bits of food, soap, or other things you sure wouldn't want in your drinking water. But you can still reuse it. A purification system can treat graywater. Then it can be used for toilets and lawns.

The state of Florida is a leader in reusing water. The state reuses 660 million gallons (2,498 million liters) of water each day. Most of the reused water is used to grow crops. Some is used to irrigate public areas like parks, golf courses, and athletic fields.

CLEAN WATER TECH

The Ultra Violet Waterworks (UVW) machine uses a 60-watt light bulb to clean 4 gallons (15 liters) of water a minute. Dirty water is placed under the light, which kills some bacteria and viruses making it an easy and cheap way to provide safe drinking water in poor countries.

Even if you don't live in Florida, you can still recycle water. Thousands of gallons of water fall on your home when it rains. The next time it does, don't let the water fall down the gutter. Recycle it! A simple way to harvest rainwater is with a rain barrel. Many towns provide them to home owners. You will conserve water. Less water will be treated. This saves energy. **How can you use rainwater? While you should never drink rainwater, it is great for:**

* Watering gardens, lawns, and house plants

* Flushing toilets

* Washing clothes

* Washing cars

* Filling bird baths

What do you call a puddle on a hot day? **Dried Up.**

XERISCAPING

XERISCAPING is a form of landscaping that's often used in dry areas. It uses local plants in the garden that need little water. It's also about using mulch and compost like shredded wood, leaves, or gravel to cover garden beds. This reduces water evaporation by protecting the soil from the sun.

BODY OF WATER

Humans need water to live. So do plants and animals. Nothing can replace water. Tap on your arm, now on your leg. They feel pretty solid, don't they? But water is inside. Your body needs about ½ gallon (2 liters) of water a day.

Imagine that your body is a large company. There are lots of important jobs to be done. Who do you want to hire to keep the company running smoothly? Let's see if water is right for the job.

Name: Water

Career Objective: Helping everything and everyone on Earth stay alive.

Special Achievements: I can be a liquid, solid, and a gas.

Skills: Within the body I digest food, take away waste, carry oxygen to the cells, make blood, keep the eyes and mouth from drying out, and control body temperature.

Sports I Like: Water sports

Clubs I Belong To: Freshwater and salt water club

Things I Like to Read: About the pioneers of hydrologic science

Hobbies: Participate in the water cycle!

Water is definitely right for the job. Congratulations, you're hired!

When you need water, your body tells you. Your mouth feels dry. You get thirsty. If your body does not get enough water, your head might hurt. You might feel tired, even cranky. You are dehydrated and you need water!

EAT WATER?

You know it is very important to drink water often. But did you know that you don't always have to drink it? You can eat water! That's right. Lots of food contains water. Here are some of them:

FOOD	WATER CONTENT
Cantaloupe	95 percent
Tomatoes	95 percent
Watermelon	92 percent
Spinach	91 percent
Milk	90 percent
Apples	85 percent

THEN+NOW

THEN: Throughout history, people have collected and carried water in buckets.

NOW: Today, some people use a Hippo Water Roller to carry water. This is a large barrel that rolls across the ground. It allows a person to carry four times as much as a bucket.

Off I Go!

Supplies

several players

obstacles such as chairs, skipping ropes, cones, etc . . .

2 cups

4 large buckets

water

Children in some parts of the world walk for hours to fetch water for their family. In this team relay, you and your friends will experience what these children do.

1. Divide players into two even teams. Set up two identical obstacle courses using chairs, skipping ropes, and other items.

2. Place one full bucket of water at the end of each course and one empty bucket at the beginning.

3. The first player from each team grabs a cup, runs through the course, and fills the cup from the end bucket. He or she runs back through the course and pours the water into the empty bucket.

4. The player tags the next person and passes the cup. This player also runs through the course, fills the cup, and runs back to empty it.

5. The team with the most water in its bucket after 5 minutes is the winner.

Your body can survive without food for weeks, but can only survive without water for a few days.

WOW!

Rain Harvester

People have been collecting and using rainwater for centuries. One method is by using hollow bamboo reeds. They direct rainwater to nearby crops.

1. Have an adult help you cut the top and bottom off four water bottles. Then cut the bottles in half, lengthwise.

2. Connect the ends using tape to make a long channel.

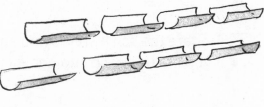

3. Tie the 8 sticks together with yarn to form four Xs. Arrange the Xs upright in a line near a garden. It should be slightly higher at one end.

4. Place the channel made from bottles on top of the Xs. At the end of the channel, place a container to harvest the rainwater. Or you can let the water drain straight into a garden. Pour some water down your channel to make sure it is not leaky.

Supplies

4 empty plastic bottles

scissors

tape

yarn

container

8 sturdy sticks of the same length

water

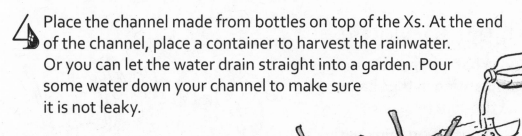

Mini Xeriscape!

Supplies

soil

mulch

plants

shovel or trowel

watering can

Gardening is fun. Ask your parents if you can make a garden. Try growing a mini container garden if you live in an apartment building.

1. Look in books, go online, or go to a garden center to research plants that grow where you live.

2. Select a few plants that don't require very much water.

3. Prepare the soil by removing any grass or weeds. If you are using a container, fill it with soil.

4. Place your plants into the soil and cover the roots. Soak the soil so the roots of the plants will grow deep to find water.

5. Cover the ground with mulch, such as leaves, to conserve moisture and enjoy!

Things to Notice

≈ **What are the advantages of planting in the shade versus the sun?**

≈ **Why do you think native plants usually need less care than plants from other areas?**

≈ **What insects or wildlife will your garden attract?**

WATER INSPIRED

EVERYONE LOVES WATER. It plays a huge role in our lives. You've learned how water supplies every living thing with life. But did you know that water is also a source of ideas?

Water inspires musicians, artists, and scientists. Musicians compose songs about water and some even use water as an instrument. Artists create sculptures and paint canvases with watery shapes and settings. Architects incorporate water-like forms into their designs. Scientists combine both art and science in new water-tech creations.

JUST **4** LAUGHS!

What did the puddle say to the raindrop?
Drop by anytime.

One exciting new area of study is called biomimicry. It's about creating technology based on ideas from nature. In Latin, *bios* means life and *mimesis* means to copy.

What are some examples of biomimicry using water?

* **bioWave and bioStream**—The bioWave is a coned-shaped device based on the swaying motion of sea plants. On the ocean floor, it transforms the energy from waves and currents into electrical energy. Meanwhile, the bioStream is a fin attached to a pole on the ocean bed. It produces energy from tidal currents. Sharks, tuna, and mackerel might want to take a second look the bioStream—its flexible fin was modeled after their tailfins!

* **Self-Cleaning Glass**—Scientists noticed that water on lotus leaves simply rolls off. So they created a self-cleaning glass that does the same thing. About 300,000 buildings in Europe already use this technology!

* **Eco Machine**—This device treats wastewater. Dirty water travels through a series of tanks that work like wetlands or marshes. Snails, small fishes, and plants are in charge of cleaning the water.

* **Glass Cactus**—A new office tower planned for Qatar doesn't just look like a glass cactus. It's heating and cooling system is based on the transpiration process of a cactus. The building's sun panels open and close to keep hot air out or let cool air in.

WATER MUSIC

You watch as large bowls of water and various kitchen tools are carried onto a stage. What is going on? It's a symphony performance by modern composer Tan Dun. He often uses water combined with traditional instruments to create his music. For example, a strainer echoes the sound of rainfall as water pours through. Amazing, unusual, and cool are all words used to describe Tan Dun's music.

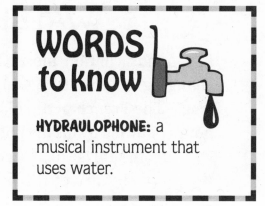

WORDS to know

HYDRAULOPHONE: a musical instrument that uses water.

Tan Dun is not the first composer to be inspired by water. George Frideric Handel and Claude Debussy also captured the whoosh, crash, drip, and roar of water in their music. The piccolo sounds like a lightning bolt. The timpani roar like thunder. The plucking of violin strings are raindrops. The piano is the waves.

HYDRAULOPHONE

Kids crowd around an iron sea serpent spraying water. It is not your usual waterpark feature. It is a musical instrument called a **HYDRAULOPHONE**. Engineering professor Steve Mann invented it. You can make music by placing your fingers over small jets of water! Blocking more than one jet makes a chord. Hydraulophones come in all shapes and sizes. There are floating ones called "Nessie" after the sea monster and large organ models. Wouldn't it be great to play in the water and make music at the same time!

WATER-INSPIRED ART

Lily ponds contain more than lilies. Their fresh scents and changing colors attract buzzing insects and curious frogs. The French artist Claude Monet spent many hours painting by his lily pond. As the hours passed from sunrise to dusk, Claude noticed how the beauty of the pond shifted as the light moved. In each painting he did of the same pond, he coated his canvases in thick brush strokes of yellow, purple, green, and white, which captured the changes of light on the water. Claude Monet's water is still, calm, and peaceful.

Modern artist Susumu Shingu is inspired by water's movements. He creates moving sculptures of snowflakes and waterfalls out of aluminum, stainless steel, and polyester cloth. These twist and turn end over end. Shingu's water is constantly changing.

Water has a different meaning for everyone. How do you see water? Is it calm like a glass of water? Is it happy like a fun day at the beach? Or do you see water as being angry like a loud thunderstorm?

Meet A Scientist

Hippocrates (460–354 BCE) invented a good way to clean rainwater for drinking. He told people to boil rainwater, and then pour it through a cloth bag, called a Hippocrates sleeve.

TALL TALES ABOUT WATER

Long ago, science was new. A lot of what people believed was not true. We now know how water moves through the water cycle and how weather happens in the atmosphere. But in the past, this was all a big mystery. So people created stories, called myths, to explain what they didn't understand about water.

Myths often featured strange creatures, gods, sea monsters, and lost cities in the ocean. Pretty scary stuff, don't you think? Read the fake newspaper headlines below to learn more about some famous water myths.

GOD OF THE SEA STRIKES AGAIN—Poseidon, ruler of the sea, is angry again. He caused last month's storm, tidal wave, and earthquake. Meet at his temple today to offer a gift. Remember, a happy Poseidon creates new land.

FISHERMAN HELPED—Nereids help another fisherman stranded at sea. These mermaid-like creatures can always be counted on. If you are new to the area, there are 50 nereids.

FROG DRINKS WATER—Yesterday a frog swallowed all of Earth's water. Luckily, the other animals made the frog laugh, forcing him to spit out all the water.

SEA MONSTER SIGHTED—Sailors report seeing a monster swimming in dark waters. It has snake-like arms, a face like a horse, and the body of a whale. It can not only pull a man overboard—it can bring an entire ship down!

HOW DO YOU SAY WATER?

There are over 6,000 languages in the world. All of them have a word for water!

Spanish, *agua*

Japanese, *mizu*

French, *eau*

Hungarian, *viz*

German, *wasser*

Chinese, *shouei*

Vietnamese, *nuoc*

Turkish, *su*

CELEBRATE!

Water is celebrated around the world through fireworks, boat races, dancing, and religious customs. Every year in Cambodia, millions of people come to a three-day water festival to celebrate the end of the rainy season. In Thailand, Songkran is the New Year water festival. People throw water at everyone and everything to wash away bad luck. They use buckets, garden hoses, and water balloons. No one is safe!

Besides ancient traditions, there are new festivals too. These stress conserving water. For example, in 1992 the United Nations wanted to raise public awareness about the one billion people worldwide who don't have enough drinking water. So they declared March 22 to be World Water Day. On that day, nations organize films, concerts, photo contests, and walk-a-thons. This year, look for an event near you—or organize your own!

> The Colorado River Aqueduct is one of the longest in the world. It is 242 miles long (389 kilometers).

WOW!

Be A Mimic

Your challenge is to design a product to solve a water problem, such as a leaky tap. Your idea must be based on something you observe in nature.

1. Go for a walk in your neighborhood or park.

2. Take note of animals. How do they move? What do they eat? Where do they live?

3. Take note of plants. What are the shapes of their leaves? Do they have seed pods?

4. For each note, take a photograph or draw a picture.

5. Put all your ideas together to complete your design. How will you encourage people to use your design?

Supplies

- notebook
- pencil
- binoculars
- flashlight
- camera
- crayons

CLEAN WATER TECH

The Aqueduct Tricycle is for adults. It carries water. When the rider pedals, the Aqueduct Tricycle filters the water!

Waterfall Sculpture

In this project you will make a waterfall sculpture that you can hang inside. Watch as air currents bring your piece to life.

1 Cut the newsprint into 15 thin vertical strips of different lengths. Roll the strips on a pencil so it curls.

2 Use colored paper to create small spirals. Tape fishing wire to the back of each piece.

3 Connect the finished shapes to the coat hanger and position them to your liking.

4 Hang up the hanger outside or by an open window. Watch as the air makes your waterfall come to life.

Supplies

newsprint

scissors

pencil

colored paper

fishing wire

tape

wire coat hanger

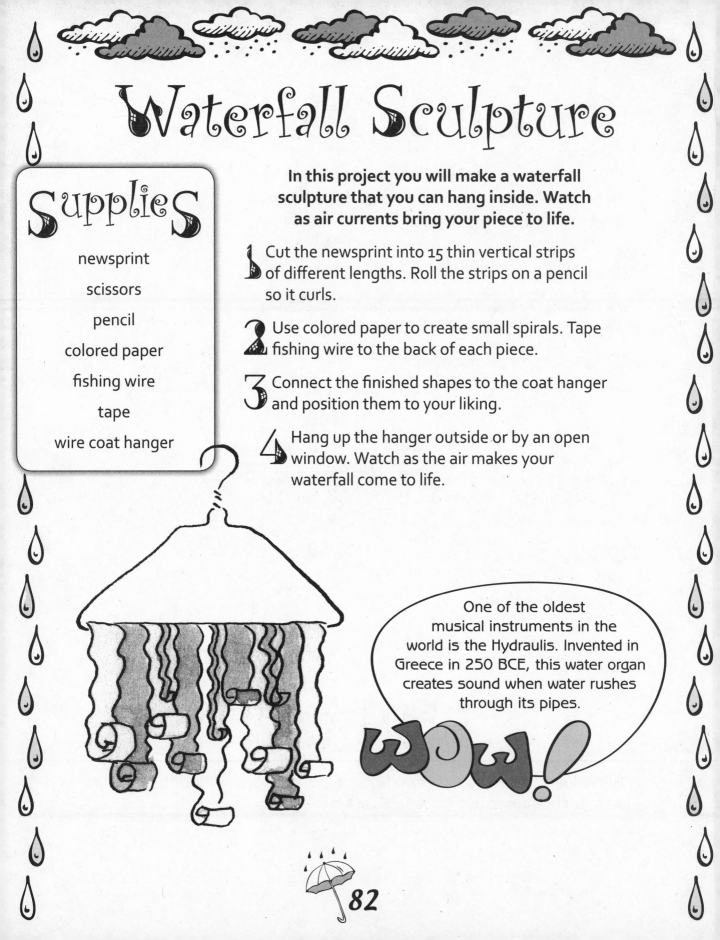

One of the oldest musical instruments in the world is the Hydraulis. Invented in Greece in 250 BCE, this water organ creates sound when water rushes through its pipes.

WOW!

Water Symphony

Composer George Frideric Handel wrote a symphony called "Water Music." It became one of his most famous pieces. He first performed "Water Music" on July 17, 1717 for the king of England, King George I, and other important people. In this activity, you are going to create your own water music using natural water sounds!

Supplies

tape recorder or recording computer program with microphone

1. Look for moving water in your home, school, or community. Is there a rushing brook? How about a fountain? What does water running in the sink sound like?

2. Tape the different water sounds. Then play them back and try to identify each sound.

Variation

≈ Do you play an instrument? Accompany the natural water sounds with music that you create.

AQUEDUCT: a network of channels used to direct water over long distances.

AQUIFER: an underground layer of rock that has space in it that holds water.

ATMOSPHERE: all of the air around the earth.

ATOM: the smallest unit of an element.

BIODEGRADABLE: can be broken down by nature.

CAPILLARY ACTION: the way water pulls itself up into another material.

CISTERN: an underground well used for storing water.

CLIMATE: average weather patterns in an area over a long period of time.

COMET: a ball of ice and dust that orbits the sun.

CONTINENT: a large land mass.

CONDENSATION: when water vapor changes to liquid.

CONSERVE: to use something carefully, so it isn't used up.

CROP: a plant grown for food or other uses.

CRUDE OIL: thick, natural oil.

CURRENT: the constant movement of water in a direction.

DENSE: packed tightly.

DEW POINT: the temperature at which water condenses into dew.

DROUGHT: a long period of time without rain.

ECOSYSTEM: a community of plants and animals living in an area, relying on each other to survive.

ELEMENT: a pure substance that contains only one kind of atom.

EQUATOR: an invisible line circling the globe, halfway between the North and South Poles.

EROSION: the wearing down of the earth's surface.

EVAPORATION: when a liquid heats up and changes to a gas.

GEOTHERMAL: a form of heat energy from the earth's core.

GLACIER: a huge mass of ice and snow.

GREENHOUSE GAS: a gas in the atmosphere that traps heat. We need some greenhouse gases, but too many trap too much heat.

GRAYWATER: water that has been used for things like laundry or washing dishes.

GROUNDWATER: underground water found in aquifers.

HUMIDITY: the amount of moisture in the air.

HYDRAULOPHONE: a musical instrument that uses water.

HYDROELECTRICITY: electricity created from falling water.

HYDROLOGIST: a person who studies water.

ICE CAP: a thick layer of permanent ice.

IRRIGATION: transporting water through canals or tunnels to water crops.

MATTER: anything that takes up space and has mass.

METEOR: a rock that orbits the sun.

METEOROLOGIST: a scientist who studies weather patterns.

METEOROLOGY: the study of weather and climate.

MIGRATION: when animals move from one area to another.

MOLECULE: a group of atoms bound together to form matter.

NITROGEN OXIDE: a colorless gas or liquid that adds to air pollution and acid rain.

NON-BIODEGRADABLE: cannot be broken down by nature.

NON-RENEWABLE: something you can run out of.

ORBIT: circle around something.

PERCOLATE: to soak through.

PH SCALE: a scale that measures acids.

PHOSPHORUS: a chemical.

POLLUTION: man-made waste that dirties an environment.

PRECIPITATION: falling moisture in the form of rain, sleet, snow, and hail.

PRECYCLE: reducing waste by purchasing a product with less packaging—or not buying it at all.

QUANAT: an underground water tunnel.

GLOSSARY

RENEWABLE RESOURCE: a substance like water that goes through the same cycle again and again. It doesn't get used up.

RESERVOIR: an area that holds water.

RUNOFF: water that flows off the land.

SATURATED ZONE: an underground area filled with water.

SHADUF: a water-lifting device.

SULFUR DIOXIDE: a colorless gas or liquid that adds to air pollution and acid rain.

SURFACE TENSION: when water molecules on the surface pull together, creating tension.

TRANSPIRATION: when water from plant leaves is released into the air.

TURBINE: a machine with rotating blades that changes one type of energy into another.

UNSATURATED ZONE: an underground area that contains soil and air.

WATER CYCLE: the natural recycling of water through evaporation, condensation, precipitation, and collection.

WATER TREATMENT PLANT: a place where water is cleaned.

WATER VAPOR: water as a gas, like steam or mist.

WATER WHEEL: a wheel with paddles attached that spins when water flows over it. The energy can be used to power machines or lift water.

WATERSHED: an area that drains into a waterway.

WATERWAY: a channel of water such as a stream or river.

WEATHER FORECAST: to predict what the weather will be.

XERISCAPING: gardening with native plants and less water.

BOOKS

Hooper, Meredith, and Chris Coady. *The Drop in My Drink: The Story of Water on our Planet.* France Lincoln Children's Books, 2008.

Jimenez, Nuria, and Empar Jimenez, *Splash! (Taking Care of you Planet)* Barron's Educational Series, 2010.

Kalman, Bobbie. *The Water Cycle.* Crabtree Publishing Company, 2006.

Latham, Donna. *Oceans.* Nomad Press, 2010.

McKinney, Barbara. *A Drop Around the World.* Dawn Publications, 1998.

Strauss, Rochelle. One Well: The Story of Water on Earth. Kids Can Press, 2007.

Walter, Wick. *A Drop of Water.* Scholastic Press, 1997.

WEB SITES

Brain Pop-Water
http://www.brainpop.com/science/earthsystem/water/preview.wemillilters

ECO Kids
http://www.ecokids.ca/pub/eco_info/topics/water/water/index.cfm

EPA Environmental Kids
http://www.epa.gov/kids/water.htm

Planet Pals
http://www.planetpals.com/weather.htmillilters

USGS Water Calculator
http://ga.water.usgs.gov/edu/sq3.htmillilters

Water Conservation around the House
http://www.ecokids.ca/

Water Cycle Stages-Puzzle
http://www.fergusonfoundation.org/hbf/watercycle/watercycle_puzzle2.shtmillilters

Water Use It Wisely
http://www.wateruseitwisely.com/kids/index.php

Weather Wiz Kids
http://www.weatherwizkids.com

World Water Day
http://www.unwater.org/worldwaterday/about.htmillilters

Quiz Your Noodle
http://kids.nationalgeographic.com/kids/games/puzzlesquizzes/quizyournoodle-water/

DOCUMENTARIES

Liquid Assets: The Story of Our Water Infrastructure (Public Television Documentary, 2008)

SCIENCE MUSEUMS, AQUARIUMS, AND SCIENCE CENTERS

American Museum of Natural History
New York, New York
www.amnh.org/exhibitions/water/

Arizona Science Center
Phoenix, Arizona
www.azscience.org/

California Science Center
Los Angeles, California
www.californiasciencecenter.org/

Connecticut Science Center
Hartford, Connecticut
www.ctsciencecenter.org/

Miami Science Museum
Miami, Florida
www.miamisci.org/

Orpheum Children's Science Museum
Champaign, Illinois
www.orpheumkids.com/

The Carnegie Science Museum
Pittsburgh, Pennsylvania
www.carnegiesciencecenter.org/

The Franklin Institute
Philadelphia, Pennsylvania
www2.fi.edu/

Scripps Institution of Oceanography
San Diego, California
www.scripps.ucsd.edu

Virginia Institute of Marine Science
Gloucester Point, Virginia
www.vims.edu/

INDEX

INDEX

E

Earth
  formation of, 2–3
  water on, 1, 2–3, 20–21
Egyptians, 27, 41, 42, 44, 51
energy/electricity, 45–49, 76
environmental issues.
  See also conservation; pollution
erosion, 3, 26, 45
evaporation, 21, 22, 33, 57, 69

F

festivals, 80
flotation, 14
food, water in, 71
Franklin, Ben, 48
freshwater, 6, 8, 59.
  See also drinking water; groundwater;
  lakes and ponds; rivers and streams
frozen water, 6–7, 12, 13.
  See also glaciers; ice/ice caps/icebergs;
  snow/sleet/hail

G

garbage, 54, 59–60
geothermal energy, 45
glaciers, 6–7, 10, 13, 21, 46
graywater, 68
Greeks, 14, 40, 42, 45, 46, 50, 82
greenhouse gases, 15.
  See also water vapor
groundwater, 6, 15, 25–26

H

hail, 24.
  See also snow/sleet/hail
Halley, Edmond, 57
Handel, George Frideric, 77, 83
Hippocrates, 78
Howard, Luke, 34
human body, water for, 70–71, 72.
  See also drinking water
humidity, 32, 38–39
hydrologists, 2, 57
hydropower/hydroelectricity, 46–48, 76

I

ice/ice caps/icebergs, 6–7, 12, 13, 33
inspiration, water as source of, 75–83
irrigation, 43, 44, 50, 51, 68, 73

L

lakes and ponds, 6, 8, 21, 22, 25, 57
litter, 54, 59–60

M

Mariana Trench, 5
meteorologists, 7, 23, 26, 35, 36
music, 75, 77, 82, 83
myths, 79

INDEX

W

X